DATE DUE

SNOW WHITE AND
THE DWARFS

Afterword by:
Betty Jane Wagner
Chair, Humanities Division
National College of Education

Copyright © 1991 Steck-Vaughn Company

Copyright © 1980, Macdonald-Raintree, Inc.

Library of Congress Number: 79-28431

7 8 9 10 11   95 94 93 92 91

Library of Congress Cataloging in Publication Data

Daniels, Patricia.
  Snow White and the dwarfs.

  (Raintree fairy tales)
  Based on Schneewittchen by the brothers Grimm.
  SUMMARY: Retells the tale of the beautiful princess
whose lips were red as blood, skin was white as snow,
and hair was black as ebony.
  [1. Fairy tales. 2. Folklore — Germany]
I. Spalding, Tony. II. Grimm, Jakob Ludwig Karl,
1785-1863. Schneewittchen. III. Title. IV. Series.
PZ8.D188Sn   398.2'2'0943 [E]   79-28431
ISBN 0-8393-0251-7 lib. bdg.

SNOW WHITE AND THE DWARFS

Retold by Patricia Daniels
Illustrated by Tony Spalding

RAINTREE
STECK-VAUGHN
L I B R A R Y
A Division of Steck-Vaughn Company

On a winter's day, long ago, a young queen sat sewing at a high window. She pricked her finger with the needle, and three drops of blood fell onto the snow outside.

When she saw this, she said, "I wish I had a daughter with lips as red as blood, skin as white as snow, and hair as black as this ebony window frame."

Her wish was granted, and she soon had a daughter with ebony-black hair, blood-red lips and snow-white skin. They called her Snow White.

The young queen died, and the king married again. The new queen was beautiful, but also evil and vain. She had a magic mirror, and looked in it every day.

E ach day the queen would ask the mirror:
"Mirror, mirror, hanging there,
Who in all the land's most fair?"
And the mirror would answer:
"You are most fair, my lady Queen,
The fairest in the land, I ween."
This made the queen happy.

When Snow White was seven years old, the queen asked the mirror her usual question. But this time it said:

"My Lady Queen, you are fair, 'tis true,
But Snow White is fairer far than you."

The queen was enraged. She called her chief huntsman to her and told him to take Snow White into the forest, kill her, and bring back her heart as proof.

T he huntsman sadly took Snow White into the forest. But when she saw the knife, she cried out:

"Please spare me! I will run away and never return!"

The huntsman took pity on her and let her run away. He killed a wild boar in the woods and took its heart to the queen instead of Snow White's.

Night filled the woods with darkness as Snow White ran. She was afraid of the strange animal noises she heard around her.

Then, in the distance, she saw the lights of a little house. When she came to it, she went in and saw a small table with seven tiny plates, and in the next room seven child-sized beds.

Snow White crawled onto one of the beds
and fell asleep.

When she awoke, she saw to her
surprise seven dwarfs standing around the bed
looking at her. At first she was afraid, but they
were very kind to her. When they heard her
story, the dwarfs told her she should stay
with them.

Snow White agreed to look after the cottage
while they were gone to work in their mines.
She was not to let anyone into the house, for
fear the queen would find out where she was.

Meanwhile, the queen had found out from her
mirror that Snow White still lived. She was
furious. She would find a way to kill Snow
White herself.

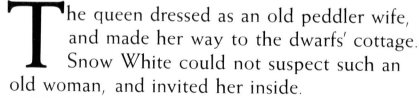

The queen dressed as an old peddler wife, and made her way to the dwarfs' cottage. Snow White could not suspect such an old woman, and invited her inside.

"You're a kind girl," said the old woman. "I will give you these bright laces to tie your bodice up." And she laced the bodice so tightly that Snow White could not breathe, and fell to the ground.

When the dwarfs returned, they saw Snow White lying on the ground as if dead. Quickly they cut the laces, and Snow White awoke. They warned her never to let anyone in.

The queen's mirror told her that Snow White was still alive. This time she prepared a poisoned comb.

When Snow White saw the little old woman at the door, she could not believe the woman would hurt her. But as soon as the comb touched her hair, she fell to the ground as if dead.

When the dwarfs came home, they searched her until they found the comb and pulled it from her hair. "Never let a stranger in again," they told her as she awoke.

Again the angry queen found out Snow White was still living. Her evil mind thought of the best plan of all. Dressed as a peasant woman, she brought a poisoned apple to Snow White's cottage. Snow White would not let her in or take the apple.

"Do not fear, child," said the witch. "See, I will eat it too." And she took a bite from the unpoisoned side of the apple.

Snow White then bit into the poisoned side of the apple. At once she fell to the ground, lifeless. The queen laughed, knowing that this time she had won.

The dwarfs wept as they tried to rouse Snow White, but nothing could move her. Because she still looked so lovely, they did not bury her. Instead they placed her in a glass coffin and set it out in the forest where they could keep watch over it.

Time passed, and Snow White seemed to grow more beautiful than ever. One day a prince rode by and saw her. Once he had seen her he felt he could not be parted from her. The dwarfs finally agreed to let him take the coffin away with him. As he lifted it, the piece of poisoned apple fell from Snow White's lips and she awoke.

The prince explained to Snow White what had happened. She agreed to go with him and be his wife.

The evil queen was dressed to go to a wedding, and asked the mirror:

"Mirror, mirror, hanging there,
Who in all the land's most fair?"

Imagine her surprise when the mirror said:

"My Lady Queen, you are fair, 'tis true,
But Snow White is fairer far than you."
At that the Queen became so angry that she
choked and died.

Now Snow White was safe. She and the
prince were married and lived happily
together. They never forgot the kindness of the
seven dwarfs.

With your finger follow the path Snow White must take to the dwarfs' cottage. Some clues from the story will help you on your way.

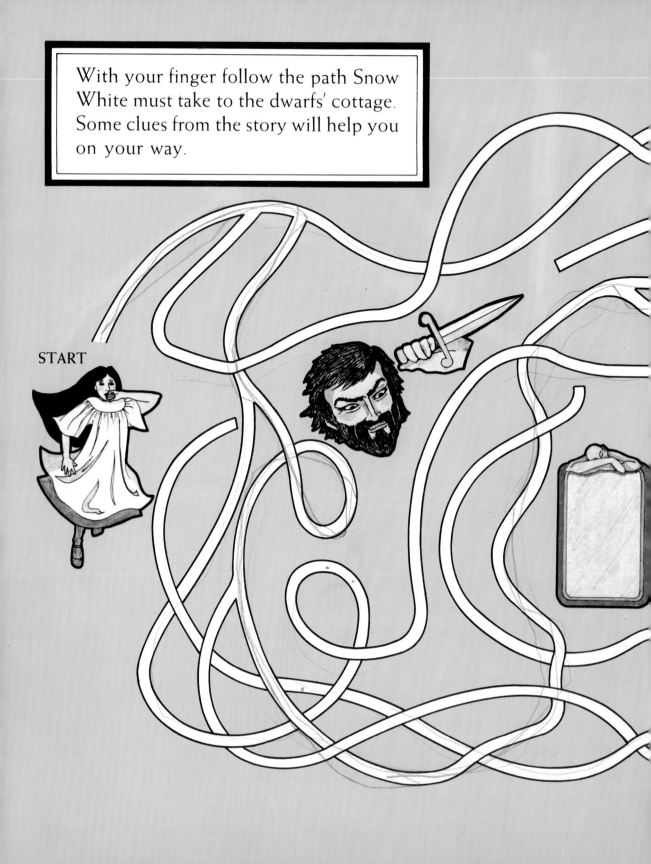

START

FINISH

(For the answer, turn to the last page.)

The Story of Snow White and The Dwarfs

"Snow White", like all folk tales, was told for hundreds of years before it was ever written down. No one knows who first made it up, but someone who heard it retold it to someone younger, and that person grew up and told it again. So the story lived even after the storyteller died.

About 175 years ago, two brothers, Jacob and Wilhelm Grimm, began collecting old German tales. They listened to an old woman of the village, Frau Katerina Viehmann, and others tell "Snow White" and wrote down their words. They published "Snow White" as part of a very important collection of German folk tales called *Household Tales*. There are many versions of this story. You might enjoy these:

- *Snow White and the Seven Dwarfs*, retold and illustrated by Dick Bruna (Follett 1966).
- *Snow White and the Seven Dwarfs*, freely translated and illustrated by Wanda Gag (Coward McCann, Inc. 1938).
- *Snow White* by the Brothers Grimm, freely translated from the German by Paul Heins, illustrated by Trina Schart Hyman (Little, Brown & Co. 1974).
- *Snow White and the Seven Dwarfs*, a tale from the Brothers Grimm, translated by Randall Jarrell, illustrated by Nancy Ekholm Burkert (Farrar, Straus and Giroux 1972).

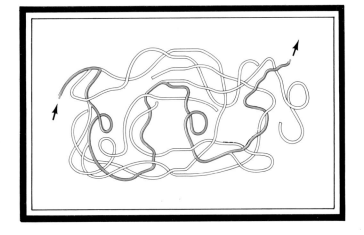